Disney's

Family Storybook Library

When the Right Thing Is Hard to Do

Stories About Fairness and Judgment

BOOK TEN

First Edition
1 3 5 7 9 10 8 6 4 2

ISBN: 0-7868-5875-3

"Friendship Blooms" is based on the edition containing the full text of *Bambi,
A Life in the Woods* by Felix Salten, published by Simon & Schuster.

When the Right Thing Is Hard to Do

Stories About Fairness and Judgment

Introduction

How boring the world would be if we were all the same! If we wore the same clothes, ate the same food, and listened to the same music, there would then be nothing new to discover and enjoy! Life is a rich tapestry, woven together by people with very different cultures and beliefs. Despite all this difference, however, people the world over need the same simple things: food, shelter, clothing, and the love of family and friends. Are we really so different after all?

Pocahontas and Captain John Smith find friendship in the most unlikely place—with each other! Likewise, because Bambi hasn't learned to dislike skunks, he makes a new friend in Flower. Friendship rules supreme!

Colors
of the Wind

from Pocahontas

The only wrong way to live is with contempt for others.

Captain John Smith was a brave explorer. His shipmates admired him for his courage and heart. They all tried to follow his example, and listened in awe to everything he told them about his many adventures. Most of all, the Captain was known as a fearless Indian fighter.

"Indians are savages," John Smith explained to his friends. "They need us to teach them the proper way to live." The Captain believed that the way of the English was the only right way to live.

When John Smith's ship landed in the New World, he decided to set out in search of hostile Indians. He walked carefully through the woods, listening and looking for them. What he didn't know was that a young Indian woman was watching him, too. Her name was Pocahontas.

John Smith came to a waterfall. There in the mist, he saw her. Pocahontas faced him bravely. He had never seen anyone so beautiful before. As he started to approach her, she turned and ran.

"Wait!" he called, running after her. "Please, I won't hurt you!

"I'm John Smith," he said, offering

his hand. He felt drawn to this lovely young woman.

"I'm Pocahontas," she said. Pocahontas had never seen an Englishman before. He was dressed in strange clothing, and carried such odd things with him. John Smith showed her his compass and musket and helmet. He explained that they were necessary for taming wild savages.

"Savages?" Pocahontas was furious. "You mean . . . like me?"

John Smith suddenly realized that he was wrong about Indians. There was nothing wild or savage about Pocahontas. She was smart and strong and proud. Surely her people were the same way. He began to feel ashamed about the things he had said.

Pocahontas took John Smith's hand and told him of her love for the earth and all the creatures in it. She spoke of the colors of the wind

until he could see them, too. For the first time, he saw that there was more than one way to live.

"Thank you," John Smith told Pocahontas humbly, "for showing me a new path." With a promise to meet her again soon, he went to tell his English friends about what he had learned.

Friendship Blooms

from *Bambi*

⎯⎯⎯ ⚬⚬⚬ ⎯⎯⎯

A few kind words can change everything.

Bambi, a newborn fawn, was curious about everything. His friend Thumper, a young rabbit, was eager to show him the world.

Wherever Bambi went in the forest,
animals greeted him. "Good morning, young
prince!" they called.

Suddenly a small golden creature danced
before Bambi's eyes. Startled, Bambi watched
it flit about. He chased the creature as it

darted ahead. Finally, it landed on Bambi's tail.

"Bird!" proclaimed Bambi.

Thumper had introduced him to a bird only moments before.

"No, that's not a bird," Thumper said. "That's a *butterfly*."

"Butterfly?" Bambi whispered to himself. There were so many words to learn.

Bambi turned to look at the butterfly again, but it had flown away. He looked around, and thought he'd found it.

"Butterfly!" he cried at a golden, soft thing on the ground. He was sure it was a butterfly!

But Thumper laughed. "No, that's a *flower*!"

"Flower," said Bambi, tasting the word.

"Uh-huh," said Thumper, showing Bambi how to sniff one. "It's *pretty*," he said.

"Pretty," Bambi
repeated, and he
bent again to the
flower patch, sniffing
deeply. A lovely,
sweet scent filled his
nostrils and tingled
through his whole
body. What a
wonderful new
sensation!

Suddenly one of
the flowers twitched,
and Bambi's nose
touched the nose of
a young skunk.

"Flower!" cried
Bambi happily to the

black-and-white creature.

"Me?" said the skunk in surprise. No one had ever called him a flower before.

Thumper burst out laughing. Imagine calling something as stinky as a skunk a flower!

"No, no, no!" Thumper cried, correcting Bambi. "That's not a flower. He's a little—"

The skunk cut him off. "Oh, that's all right," the skunk said. "He can call me a flower if he wants to!" The skunk giggled. "I don't mind a bit!"

The skunk had never felt so warm and happy inside. He was a shy animal, and used to being shunned by strangers.

"Pretty, pretty flower!" Bambi exclaimed.

"Oh, gosh," said the skunk, and he laughed softly.

From then on, Bambi, Thumper, and Flower were the best of friends.